Mr Bunny's Chocolate Factory

ELYS DOLAN

For chickens, thanks for all the eggs.
Also Emma, Ellen, and Sarah because of benchminton.

OXFORD
UNIVERSITY PRESS

Great Clarendon Street, Oxford OX2 6DP
Oxford University Press is a department of the University of Oxford.
It furthers the University's objective of excellence in research, scholarship,
and education by publishing worldwide. Oxford is a registered trade mark of
Oxford University Press in the UK and in certain other countries

Text and illustrations copyright © Elys Dolan 2017

The moral rights of the author and illustrator have been asserted
Database right Oxford University Press (maker)

First published 2017

Data available

ISBN: 978-0-19-274619-1 (hardback)
ISBN: 978-0-19-274620-7 (paperback)
ISBN: 978-019-27-4621-4 (eBook)

1 3 5 7 9 10 8 6 4 2

Printed in China

Paper used in the production of this book is a natural, recyclable
product made from wood grown in sustainable forests.
The manufacturing process conforms to the environmental
regulations of the country of origin.

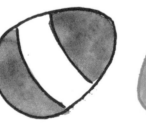

How Do You THINK CHOCOLATE EGGS ARE MADE?

Well, there is a factory . . .

Mr Bunnys
CHOCOLATE
FACTORY

. . . run by a bunny (that's Mr Bunny to you).

MR BUNNY

Mr Bunny was selling a lot of chocolate eggs and getting very rich . . .

But he still wasn't satisfied.

Mr Bunny ordered the chickens to crank chocolate production up to the max.

Mr Bunny forced the chickens to eat and eat and eat . . .
EAT IT.
I can't squeeze any more out!
But we've not met our quota!
CONVEYER CONTROL
Why are the eggs not coming down?
There's another case of severe tummy ache up on the laying floor.

They were laying so many eggs
that the wrappers just couldn't keep up.

Soon Edgar was finding more bad eggs than ever.

But the chickens weren't going to take it any more.

With the chickens gone, Mr Bunny and Edgar got straight to work...

But even Edgar couldn't go on working with Mr Bunny for long.

So, Mr Bunny ate . . .

and he ate . . .

and he ate . . .

SQUEEZE!

. . . but it just didn't feel right.

Soon, Mr Bunny started to think that MAYBE he couldn't run the factory all by himself.

Mr Bunny was a very sorry rabbit...

Mr Bunny promised to try doing things a different way.

And soon he was a changed rabbit.

It's the chocolate Mr Bunnys,
which remind him why you shouldn't be a bad egg.